LUCIAN'S TRUE HISTORY

LUCIAN OF SAMOSATA

© 2020 by LUCIAN OF SAMOSATA (Public Domain)
Edition : Les prairies numériques
ISBN : 9782491251697
Legal deposit : August 2020

All rights reserved

Even as champions and wrestlers and such as practise the strength and agility of body are not only careful to retain a sound constitution of health, and to hold on their ordinary course of exercise, but sometimes also to recreate themselves with seasonable intermission, and esteem it as a main point of their practice; so I think it necessary for scholars and such as addict themselves to the study of learning, after they have travelled long in the perusal of serious authors, to relax a little the intention of their thoughts, that they may be more apt and able to endure a continued course of study.

And this kind of repose will be the more conformable, and fit their purpose better, if it be employed in the reading of such works as shall not only yield a bare content by the pleasing and comely composure of them, but shall also give occasion of some learned speculation to the mind, which I suppose I have effected in these books of mine: wherein not only the novelty of the subject, nor the pleasingness of the project, may tickle the reader with delight, nor to hear so many notorious lies delivered persuasively and in the way of truth, but because everything here by me set down doth in a comical fashion glance at some or other of the old poets, historiographers, and philosophers, which in their writings have recorded many monstrous and intolerable untruths, whose names I would have quoted down, but that I knew the reading would bewray them to you.

Ctesias, the son of Ctesiochus, the Cnidian, wrote of the region of the Indians and the state of those countries, matters which he neither saw himself, nor ever heard come from the mouth of any man. Iambulus also wrote many strange miracles of the great sea, which all men knew to be lies and fictions, yet so composed that they want not their delight: and many others have made choice of the like argument, of which some have published their own travels and peregrinations, wherein they have described the greatness of beasts, the fierce condition of men, with their strange and uncouth manner of life: but the first father and founder of all this foolery was Homer's Ulysses, who tells a long tale to Alcinous of the servitude of the winds, and of wild men with one eye in their foreheads that fed upon raw flesh, of beasts with many heads, and the transformation of his friends by enchanted potions, all which he made the silly Phæakes believe for great sooth.

This coming to my perusal, I could not condemn ordinary men for lying, when I saw it in request amongst them that would be counted philosophical persons: yet could not but wonder at them, that, writing so manifest lies, they should not think to be taken with the manner; and this made me also ambitious to leave some monument of myself behind me, that I might not be the only man exempted from this liberty of lying: and because I had no matter of verity to employ my pen in (for nothing hath befallen me worth the writing), I turned my style to publish untruths, but with an honester mind than others have done: for this one thing I confidently pronounce for a truth, that I lie: and this, I hope, may be an excuse for all the rest, when I confess what I am faulty in: for I write of matters which I neither saw nor suffered, nor heard by report from others, which are in no being, nor possible ever to have a beginning. Let no man therefore in any case give any credit to them.

Disanchoring on a time from the pillars of Hercules, the wind fitting me well for my purpose, I thrust into the West Ocean. The occasion that moved me to take such a voyage in hand was only a curiosity of mind, a desire of novelties, and a longing to learn out the bounds of the ocean, and what people inhabit the farther shore: for which purpose I made plentiful provision of victuals and fresh water, got fifty companions of the same humour to associate me in my travels, furnished myself with store of munition, gave a round sum of money to an expert pilot that could direct us in our course, and new rigged and repaired a tall ship strongly to hold a tedious and difficult journey.

Thus sailed we forward a day and a night with a prosperous wind, and as long as we had any sight of land, made no great haste on our way; but the next morrow about sun rising the wind blew high and the waves began to swell and a darkness fell upon us, so that we could not see to strike our sails, but gave our ship over to the wind and weather; thus were we tossed in this tempest the space of threescore and nineteen days together. On the fourscorth day the sun upon a sudden brake out, and we descried not far off us an island full of mountains and woods, about the which the seas did not rage so boisterously, for the storm was now reasonably well calmed: there we thrust in and went on shore and cast ourselves upon the ground, and so lay a long time, as utterly tired with our misery at sea: in the end we arose up and divided ourselves: thirty we left to guard our ship: myself and twenty more went to discover the island, and had not gone above three furlongs from the sea through a wood, but we saw a brazen pillar erected, whereupon Greek letters were engraven, though now much worn and hard to be discerned, importing, "Thus far travelled Hercules and Bacchus."

There were also near unto the place two portraitures cut out in a rock, the one of the quantity of an acre of ground, the other less, which made me imagine the lesser to be Bacchus and the other Hercules: and giving them due adoration, we proceeded on our journey, and far we had not gone but we came to a river, the stream whereof seemed to run with as rich wine as any is made in Chios, and of a great breadth, in some places able to bear a ship, which made me to give the more credit to the inscription upon the pillar, when I saw such apparent signs of Bacchus's peregrination. We then resolved to travel up the stream to find whence the river had his original, and when we were come to the head, no spring at all appeared, but mighty great vine-trees of infinite number, which from their roots distilled pure wine which made the river run so abundantly: the stream was also well stored with fish, of which we took a few, in taste and colour much resembling wine, but as many as ate of them fell drunk upon it; for when they were opened and cut up, we found them to be full of lees: afterwards we mixed some fresh water fish with them, which allayed the strong taste of the wine. We then crossed the stream where we found it passable, and came among a world of vines of incredible number, which towards the earth had firm stocks and of a good growth; but the tops of them were women, from the hip upwards, having all their proportion perfect and complete; as painters picture out Daphne, who was turned into a tree when she was overtaken by Apollo; at their fingers' ends sprung out branches full of grapes, and the hair of their heads was nothing else but winding wires and leaves, and clusters of grapes. When we were come to them, they saluted us and joined hands with us, and spake unto us some in the Lydian and some in the Indian language, but most of them in Greek: they also kissed us with their mouths, but he that was so kissed fell drunk, and was not his own man a good while after: they could not abide to have any fruit pulled from them, but would roar and cry out pitifully if any man offered it. Some of them desired to have carnal mixture with us, and two of our company were so bold as to entertain their offer, and could never afterwards be loosed from them, but were knit fast together at their nether parts, from whence they grew together and took root together, and their fingers began to spring out with branches and crooked wires as if they were ready to bring out fruit: whereupon we forsook them and fled to our ships, and told the company at our coming what had betide unto us, how our fellows were entangled, and of their copulation with the vines. Then we took certain of our vessels and filled them, some with water and some with wine out of the river, and lodged for that night near the shore.

On the morrow we put to sea again, the wind serving us weakly, but about noon, when we had lost sight of the island, upon a sudden a whirlwind caught us, which turned our ship round about, and lifted us up some three thousand furlongs into the air, and suffered us not to settle again into the sea, but we hung above ground, and were carried aloft with a mighty wind which filled our sails strongly. Thus for seven days' space and so many nights were we driven along in that manner, and on the eighth day we came in view of a great country in the air, like to a shining island, of a round proportion, gloriously glittering with light, and approaching to it, we there arrived, and took land, and surveying the country, we found it to be both inhabited and husbanded: and as long as the day lasted we could see nothing there, but when night was come many other islands appeared unto us, some greater and some less, all of the colour of fire, and another kind of earth underneath, in which were cities and seas and rivers and woods and mountains, which we conjectured to be the earth by us inhabited: and going further into the land, we were met withal and taken by those kind of people which they call Hippogypians. These Hippogypians are men riding upon monstrous vultures, which they use instead of horses: for the vultures there are exceeding great, every one with three heads apiece: you may imagine their greatness by this, for every feather in their wings was bigger and longer than the mast of a tall ship: their charge was to fly about the country, and all the strangers they found to bring them to the king: and their fortune was then to seize upon us, and by them we were presented to him. As soon as he saw us, he conjectured by our habit what countrymen we were, and said, Are not you, strangers, Grecians? which when we affirmed, And how could you make way, said he, through so much air as to get hither?

Then we delivered the whole discourse of our fortunes to him; whereupon he began to tell us likewise of his own adventures, how that he also was a man, by name Endymion, and rapt up long since from the earth as he was asleep, and brought hither, where he was made king of the country, and said it was that region which to us below seemed to be the moon; but he bade us be of good cheer and fear no danger, for we should want nothing we stood in need of: and if the war he was now in hand withal against the sun succeeded fortunately, we should live with him in the highest degree of happiness. Then we asked of him what enemies he had, and the cause of the quarrel: and he answered, Phaethon, the king of the inhabitants of the sun (for that is also peopled as well as the moon), hath made war against us a long time upon this occasion: I once assembled all the poor people and needy persons within my dominions, purposing to send a colony to inhabit the Morning Star, because the country was desert and had nobody dwelling in it. This Phaethon envying, crossed me in my design, and sent his Hippomyrmicks to meet with us in the midway, by whom we were surprised at that time, being not prepared for an encounter, and were forced to retire: now therefore my purpose is once again to denounce war and publish a plantation of people there: if therefore you will participate with us in our expedition, I will furnish you every one with a prime vulture and all armour answerable for service, for to-morrow we must set forwards. With all our hearts, said I, if it please you. Then were we feasted and abode with him, and in the morning arose to set ourselves in-order of battle, for our scouts had given us knowledge that the enemy was at hand. Our forces in number amounted to an hundred thousand, besides such as bare burthens and engineers, and the foot forces and the strange aids: of these, fourscore thousand were Hippogypians, and twenty thousand that rode upon Lachanopters, which is a mighty great fowl, and instead of feathers covered thick over with wort leaves; but their wing feathers were much like the leaves of lettuces: after them were placed the Cenchrobolians and the Scorodomachians: there came also to aid us from the Bear Star thirty thousand Psyllotoxotans, and fifty thousand Anemodromians: these Psyllotoxotans ride upon great fleas, of which they have their denomination, for every flea among them is as big as a dozen elephants: the Anemodromians are footmen, yet flew in the air without feathers in this manner: every man had a large mantle reaching down to his foot, which the wind blowing against, filled it like a sail, and they were carried along as if they had been boats: the most part of these in fight were targeteers. It was said also that there were expected from the stars over Cappadocia threescore and ten thousand Struthobalanians and five thousand Hippogeranians, but I had no sight of them, for they were not yet come, and therefore I durst write nothing, though wonderful and incredible reports were given out of them. This was the number of Endymion's army; the furniture was all alike; their helmets of bean hulls, which are great with them and very strong; their breastplates all of lupins cut into scales, for they take the shells of lupins, and fastening them together, make breastplates of them which are impenetrable and as hard as any horn: their shields and swords like to ours in Greece: and when the time of battle was come, they were ordered in this manner. The right wing was supplied by the Hippogypians, where the king himself was in person with the choicest soldiers in the army, among whom we also were ranged: the Lachanopters made the left wing, and the aids were placed in the main battle as every man's fortune fell: the foot, which in number were about six thousand myriads, were disposed of in this manner: there are many spiders in those parts of mighty bigness, every one in quantity exceeding one of the Islands Cyclades: these were appointed to spin a web in the air between the Moon and the Morning Star, which was done in an instant, and made a plain champaign upon which the foot forces were planted, who had for their leader Nycterion, the son of Eudianax, and two other associates.

But of the enemy's side the left wing consisted of the Hippomyrmicks, and among them Phaethon himself: these are beasts of huge bigness and winged, carrying the resemblance of our emmets, but for their greatness: for those of the largest size were of the quantity of two acres, and not only the riders supplied the place of soldiers, but they also did much mischief with their horns: they were in number fifty thousand. In the right wing were ranged the Aeroconopes, of which there were also about fifty thousand, all archers riding upon great gnats: then followed the Aerocardakes, who were light armed and footmen, but good soldiers, casting out of slings afar off huge great turnips, and whosoever was hit with them lived not long after, but died with the stink that proceeded from their wounds: it is said they use to anoint their bullets with the poison of mallows. After them were placed the Caulomycetes, men-at-arms and good at hand strokes, in number about fifty thousand: they are called Caulomycetes because their shields were made of mushrooms and their spears of the stalks of the herb asparagus: near unto them were placed the Cynobalanians, that were sent from the Dogstar to aid him: these were men with dogs' faces, riding upon winged acorns: but the slingers that should have come out of *Via Lactea*, and the Nephelocentaurs came too short of these aids, for the battle was done before their arrival, so that they did them no good: and indeed the slingers came not at all, wherefore they say Phaethon in displeasure over-ran their country. These were the forces that Phaethon brought into the field: and when they were joined in battle, after the signal was given, and when the asses on either side had brayed (for these are to them instead of trumpets), the fight began, and the left wing of the Heliotans, or Sun soldiers, fled presently and would not abide to receive the charge of the Hippogypians, but turned their backs immediately, and many were put to the sword: but the right wing of theirs were too hard for our left wing, and drove them back till they came to our footmen, who joining with them, made the enemies there also turn their backs and fly, especially when they found their own left wing to be overthrown. Thus were they wholly discomfited on all hands; many were taken prisoners, and many slain; much blood was spilt; some fell upon the clouds, which made them look of a red colour, as sometimes they appear to us about sun-setting; some dropped down upon the earth, which made me suppose it was upon some such occasion that Homer thought Jupiter rained blood for the death of his son Sarpedon. Returning from the pursuit, we erected two trophies: one for the fight on foot, which we placed upon the spiders' web: the other for the fight in the air, which we set up upon the clouds. As soon as this was done, news came to us by our scouts that the Nephelocentaurs were coming on, which indeed should have come to Phaethon before the fight. And when they drew so near unto us that we could take full view of them, it was a strange sight to behold such monsters, composed of flying horses and men: that part which resembled mankind, which was from the waist upwards, did equal in greatness the Rhodian Colossus, and that which was like a horse was as big as a great ship of burden: and of such multitude that I was fearful to set down their number lest it might be taken for a lie: and for their leader they had the Sagittarius out of the Zodiac. When they heard that their friends were foiled, they sent a messenger to Phaethon to renew the fight: whereupon they set themselves in array, and fell upon the Selenitans or the Moon soldiers that were troubled, and disordered in following the chase, and scattered in gathering the spoils, and put them all to flight, and pursued the king into his city, and killed the greatest part of his birds, overturned the trophies he had set up, and overcame the whole country that was spun by the spiders. Myself and two of my companions were taken alive. When Phaethon himself was come they set up other trophies in token of victory, and on the morrow we were carried prisoners into the Sun, our arms bound behind us with a piece of the cobweb: yet would they by no means lay any siege to the city, but returned and built up a wall in the midst of the air to keep the light of the Sun from falling upon the Moon, and they made it a double wall, wholly compact of clouds, so that a manifest eclipse of the Moon ensued, and all things detained in perpetual night: wherewith Endymion was so much oppressed that he sent ambassadors to entreat the demolishing of the building, and beseech him that he would not damn them to live in darkness, promising to pay him tribute, to be his friend and associate, and never after to stir against him. Phaethon's council twice assembled to consider upon this offer, and in their first meeting would remit nothing of their conceived displeasure, but on the morrow they altered their minds to these terms.

"The Heliotans and their colleagues have made a peace with the Selenitans and their associates upon these conditions, that the Heliotans shall cast down the wall, and deliver the prisoners that they have taken upon a ratable ransom: and that the Selenitans should leave the other stars at liberty, and raise no war against the Heliotans, but aid and assist one another if either of them should be invaded: that the king of the Selenitans should yearly pay to the king of the Heliotans in way of tribute ten thousand vessels of dew, and deliver ten thousand of their people to be pledges for their fidelity: that the colony to be sent to the Morning Star should be jointly supplied by them both, and liberty given to any else that would to be sharers in it: that these articles of peace should be engraven in a pillar of amber, to be erected in the midst of the air upon the confines of their country: for the performance whereof were sworn of the Heliotans, Pyronides and Therites and Phlogius: and of the Selenitans, Nyctor and Menius and Polylampes." Thus was the peace concluded, the wall immediately demolished, and we that were prisoners delivered. Being returned into the Moon, they came forth to meet us, Endymion himself and all his friends, who embraced us with tears, and desired us to make our abode with him, and to be partners in the colony, promising to give me his own son in marriage (for there are no women amongst them), which I by no means would yield unto, but desired of all loves to be dismissed again into the sea, and he finding it impossible to persuade us to his purpose, after seven days' feasting, gave us leave to depart.

Now, what strange novelties worthy of note I observed during the time of my abode there, I will relate unto you. The first is, that they are not begotten of women, but of mankind: for they have no other marriage but of males: the name of women is utterly unknown among them: until they accomplish the age of five and twenty years, they are given in marriage to others: from that time forwards they take others in marriage to themselves: for as soon as the infant is conceived the leg begins to swell, and afterwards when the time of birth is come, they give it a lance and take it out dead: then they lay it abroad with open mouth towards the wind, and so it takes life: and I think thereof the Grecians call it the belly of the leg, because therein they bear their children instead of a belly. I will tell you now of a thing more strange than this. There are a kind of men among them called Dendritans, which are begotten in this manner: they cut out the right stone out of a man's cod, and set it in their ground, from which springeth up a great tree of flesh, with branches and leaves, bearing a kind of fruit much like to an acorn, but of a cubit in length, which they gather when they are ripe, and cut men out of them: their privy members are to be set on and taken off as they have occasion: rich men have them made of ivory, poor men of wood, wherewith they perform the act of generation and accompany their spouses.

When a man is come to his full age he dieth not, but is dissolved like smoke and is turned into air. One kind of food is common to them all, for they kindle a fire and broil frogs upon the coals, which are with them in infinite numbers flying in the air, and whilst they are broiling, they sit round about them as it were about a table, and lap up the smoke that riseth from them, and feast themselves therewith, and this is all their feeding. For their drink they have air beaten in a mortar, which yieldeth a kind of moisture much like unto dew. They have no avoidance of excrements, either of urine or dung, neither have they any issue for that purpose like unto us. Their boys admit copulation, not like unto ours, but in their hams, a little above the calf of the leg, for there they are open. They hold it a great ornament to be bald, for hairy persons are abhorred with them, and yet among the stars that are comets it is thought commendable, as some that have travelled those coasts reported unto us. Such beards as they have are growing a little above their knees. They have no nails on their feet, for their whole foot is all but one toe. Every one of them at the point of his rump hath a long colewort growing out instead of a tail, always green and flourishing, which though a man fall upon his back, cannot be broken. The dropping of their noses is more sweet than honey. When they labour or exercise themselves, they anoint their body with milk, wherein to if a little of that honey chance to drop, it will be turned into cheese. They make very fat oil of their beans, and of as delicate a savour as any sweet ointment. They have many vines in those parts, which yield them but water: for the grapes that hang upon the clusters are like our hailstones: and I verily think that when the vines there are shaken with a strong wind, there falls a storm of hail amongst us by the breaking down of those kind of berries. Their bellies stand them instead of satchels to put in their necessaries, which they may open and shut at their pleasure, for they have neither liver nor any kind of entrails, only they are rough and hairy within, so that when their young children are cold, they may be enclosed therein to keep them warm. The rich men have garments of glass, very soft and delicate: the poorer sort of brass woven, whereof they have great plenty, which they enseam with water to make it fit for the workman, as we do our wool. If I should write what manner of eyes they have, I doubt I should be taken for a liar in publishing a matter so incredible: yet I cannot choose but tell it: for they have eyes to take in and out as please themselves: and when a man is so disposed, he may take them out and lay them by till he have occasion to use them, and then put them in and see again: many when they have lost their own eyes, borrow of others, for the rich have many lying by them. Their ears are all made of the leaves of plane-trees, excepting those that come of acorns, for they only have them made of wood.

I saw also another strange thing in the same court: a mighty great glass lying upon the top of a pit of no great depth, whereinto, if any man descend, he shall hear everything that is spoken upon the earth: if he but look into the glass, he shall see all cities and all nations as well as if he were among them. There had I the sight of all my friends and the whole country about: whether they saw me or not I cannot tell: but if they believe it not to be so, let them take the pains to go thither themselves and they shall find my words true. Then we took our leaves of the king and such as were near him, and took shipping and departed: at which time Endymion bestowed upon me two mantles made of their glass, and five of brass, with a complete armour of those shells of lupins, all which I left behind me in the whale: and sent with us a thousand of his Hippogypians to conduct us five hundred furlongs on our way. In our course we coasted many other countries, and lastly arrived at the Morning Star now newly inhabited, where we landed and took in fresh water: from thence we entered the Zodiac, passing by the Sun, and, leaving it on our right hand, took our course near unto the shore, but landed not in the country, though our company did much desire it, for the wind would not give us leave: but we saw it was a flourishing region, fat and well watered, abounding with all delights: but the Nephelocentaurs espying us, who were mercenary soldiers to Phaethon, made to our ship as fast as they could, and finding us to be friends, said no more unto us, for our Hippogypians were departed before. Then we made forwards all the next night and day, and about evening-tide following we came to a city called Lychnopolis, still holding on our course downwards. This city is seated in the air between the Pleiades and the Hyades, somewhat lower than the Zodiac, and arriving there, not a man was to be seen, but lights in great numbers running to and fro, which were employed, some in the market place, and some about the haven, of which many were little, and as a man may say, but poor things; some again were great and mighty, exceeding glorious and resplendent, and there were places of receipt for them all; every one had his name as well as men; and we did hear them speak. These did us no harm, but invited us to feast with them, yet we were so fearful, that we durst neither eat nor sleep as long as we were there. Their court of justice standeth in the midst of the city, where the governor sitteth all the night long calling every one by name, and he that answereth not is adjudged to die, as if he had forsaken his ranks. Their death is to be quenched. We also standing amongst them saw what was done, and heard what answers the lights made for themselves, and the reasons they alleged for tarrying so long: there we also knew our own light, and spake unto it, and questioned it of our affairs at home, and how all did there, which related everything unto us. That night we made our abode there, and on the next morrow returned to our ship, and sailing near unto the clouds had a sight of the city Nephelococcygia, which we beheld with great wonder, but entered not into it, for the wind was against us. The king thereof was Coronus, the son of Cottyphion: and I could not choose but think upon the poet Aristophanes, how wise a man he was, and how true a reporter, and how little cause there is to question his fidelity for what he hath written.

The third after, the ocean appeared plainly unto us, though we could see no land but what was in the air, and those countries also seemed to be fiery and of a glittering colour. The fourth day about noon, the wind gently forbearing, settled us fair and leisurely into the sea; and as soon as we found ourselves upon water, we were surprised with incredible gladness, and our joy was unexpressible; we feasted and made merry with such provision as we had; we cast ourselves into the sea, and swam up and down for our disport, for it was a calm. But oftentimes it falleth out that the change to the better is the beginning of greater evils: for when we had made only two days' sail in the water, as soon as the third day appeared, about sun-rising, upon a sudden we saw many monstrous fishes and whales: but one above the rest, containing in greatness fifteen hundred furlongs, which came gaping upon us and troubled the sea round about him, so that he was compassed on every side with froth and foam, showing his teeth afar off, which were longer than any beech trees are with us, all as sharp as needles, and as white as ivory: then we took, as we thought, our last leaves one of another, and embracing together, expected our ending day. The monster was presently with us, and swallowed us up ship and all; but by chance he caught us not between his chops, for the ship slipped through the void passages down into his entrails. When we were thus got within him we continued a good while in darkness, and could see nothing till he began to gape, and then we perceived it to be a monstrous whale of a huge breadth and height, big enough to contain a city that would hold ten thousand men: and within we found small fishes and many other creatures chopped in pieces, and the masts of ships and anchors and bones of men and luggage. In the midst of him was earth and hills, which were raised, as I conjectured, by the settling of the mud which came down his throat, for woods grew upon them and trees of all sorts and all manner of herbs, and it looked as if it had been husbanded. The compass of the land was two hundred and forty furlongs: there were also to be seen all kind of sea fowl, as gulls, halcyons and others that had made their nests upon the trees. Then we fell to weeping abundantly, but at the last I roused up my company, and propped up our ship and struck fire. Then we made ready supper of such as we had, for abundance of all sort of fish lay ready by us, and we had yet water enough left which we brought out of the Morning Star.

The next morrow we rose to watch when the whale should gape: and then looking out, we could sometimes see mountains, sometimes only the skies, and many times islands, for we found that the fish carried himself with great swiftness to every part of the sea. When we grew weary of this, I took seven of my company, and went into the wood to see what I could find there, and we had not gone above five furlongs but we light upon a temple erected to Neptune, as by the title appeared, and not far off we espied many sepulchres and pillars placed upon them, with a fountain of clear water close unto it: we also heard the barking of a dog, and saw smoke rise afar off, so that we judged there was some dwelling thereabout. Wherefore making the more haste, we lighted upon an old man and a youth, who were very busy in making a garden and in conveying water by a channel from the fountain into it: whereupon we were surprised both with joy and fear: and they also were brought into the same taking, and for a long time remained mute. But after some pause, the old man said, What are ye, you strangers? any of the sea spirits? or miserable men like unto us? for we that are men by nature, born and bred in the earth, are now sea-dwellers, and swim up and down within the Continent of this whale, and know not certainly what to think of ourselves: we are like to men that be dead, and yet believe ourselves to be alive. Whereunto I answered, For our parts, father, we are men also, newly come hither, and swallowed up ship and all but yesterday: and now come purposely within this wood which is so large and thick: some good angel, I think, did guide us hither to have the sight of you, and to make us know that we are not the only men confined within this monster: tell us therefore your fortunes, we beseech you, what you are, and how you came into this place. But he answered, You shall not hear a word from me, nor ask any more questions until you have taken part of such viands as we are able to afford you. So he took us and brought us into his house, which was sufficient to serve his turn: his pallets were prepared, and all things else made ready. Then he set before us herbs and nuts and fish, and filled out of his own wine unto us: and when we were sufficiently satisfied, he then demanded of us what fortunes we had endured, and I related all things to him in order that had betide unto us, the tempest, the passages in the island, our navigation in the air, our war, and all the rest, even till our diving into the whale. Whereat he wondered exceedingly, and began to deliver also what had befallen to him, and said, By lineage, O ye strangers, I am of the isle Cyprus, and travelling from mine own country as a merchant, with this my son you see here, and many other friends with me, made a voyage for Italy in a great ship full fraught with merchandise, which perhaps you have seen broken in pieces in the mouth of the whale. We sailed with fair weather till we were as far as Sicily, but there we were overtaken with such a boisterous storm that the third day we were driven into the ocean, where it was our fortune to meet with this whale which swallowed us all up, and only we two escaped with our lives; all the rest perished, whom we have here buried and built a temple to Neptune. Ever since we have continued this course of life, planting herbs and feeding upon fish and nuts: here is wood enough, you see, and plenty of vines which yield most delicate wine: we have also a well of excellent cool water, which it may be you have seen: we make our beds of the leaves of trees, and burn as much wood as we will: we chase after the birds that fly about us, and go out upon the gills of the monster to catch after live fishes: here we bathe ourselves when we are disposed, for we have a lake of salt water not far off, about some twenty furlongs in compass, full of sundry sorts of fish, in which we swim and sail upon it in a little boat of mine own making. This is the seven-and-twentieth year of our drowning, and with all this we might be well enough contented if our neighbours and borderers about us were not perverse and troublesome, altogether insociable and of stern condition. Is it so, indeed, said I, that there should be any within the whale but yourselves? Many, said he, and such as are unreconcilable towards strangers, and of monstrous and deformed proportions. The western countries and the tail-part of the wood are inhabited by the Tarychanians that look like eels, with faces like a lobster: these are warlike, fierce, and feed upon raw flesh: they that dwell towards the right side are called Tritonomendetans, which have their upper parts like unto men, their lower parts like cats, and are less offensive than the rest. On the left side inhabit the Carcinochirians and the Thinnocephalians, which are in league one with another: the middle region is possessed by the Paguridians, and the Psettopodians, a warlike nation and swift of foot: eastwards towards the mouth is for the most part desert, as overwashed by the sea: yet am I fain to take that for my dwelling, paying yearly to the Psettopodians in way of tribute five hundred oysters.

Of so many nations doth this country consist. We must therefore devise among ourselves either how to be able to fight with them, or how to live among them. What number may they all amount unto? said I. More than a thousand, said he. And what armour have they? None at all, said he, but the bones of fishes. Then were it our best course, said I, to encounter them, being provided as we are, and they without weapons, for if we prove too hard for them we shall afterward live out of fear. This we concluded upon, and went to our ship to furnish ourselves with arms. The occasion of war we gave by non-payment of tribute, which then was due, for they sent their messengers to demand it, to whom he gave a harsh and scornful answer, and sent them packing with their arrant. But the Psettopodians and Paguridians, taking it ill at the hands of Scintharus, for so was the man named, came against us with great tumult: and we, suspecting what they would do, stood upon our guard to wait for them, and laid five-and-twenty of our men in ambush, commanding them as soon as the enemy was passed by to set upon them, who did so, and arose out of their ambush, and fell upon the rear. We also being five-and-twenty in number (for Scintharus and his son were marshalled among us) advanced to meet with them, and encountered them with great courage and strength: but in the end we put them to flight and pursued them to their very dens. Of the enemies were slain an hundred threescore and ten, and but one of us besides Trigles, our pilot, who was thrust through the back with a fish's rib. All that day following and the night after we lodged in our trenches, and set on end a dry backbone of a dolphin instead of a trophy.

The next morrow the rest of the country people, perceiving what had happened, came to assault us. The Tarychanians were ranged in the right wing, with Pelamus their captain: the Thinnocephalians were placed in the left wing: the Carcinochirians made up the main battle: for the Tritonomendetans stirred not, neither would they join with either part. About the temple of Neptune we met with them, and joined fight with a great cry, which was answered with an echo out of the whale as if it had been out of a cave: but we soon put them to flight, being naked people, and chased them into the wood, making ourselves masters of the country. Soon after they sent ambassadors to us to crave the bodies of the dead and to treat upon conditions of peace; but we had no purpose to hold friendship with them, but set upon them the next day and put them all to the sword except the Tritonomendetans, who, seeing how it fared with the rest of their fellows, fled away through the gills of the fish, and cast themselves into the sea. Then we travelled all the country over, which now was desert, and dwelt there afterwards without fear of enemies, spending the time in exercise of the body and in hunting, in planting vineyards and gathering fruit of the trees, like such men as live delicately and have the world at will, in a spacious and unavoidable prison. This kind of life led we for a year and eight months, but when the fifth day of the ninth month was come, about the time of the second opening of his mouth (for so the whale did once every hour, whereby we conjectured how the hours went away), I say about the second opening, upon a sudden we heard a great cry and a mighty noise like the calls of mariners and the stirring of oars, which troubled us not a little. Wherefore we crept up to the very mouth of the fish, and standing within his teeth, saw the strangest sight that ever eye beheld—men of monstrous greatness, half a furlong in stature, sailing upon mighty great islands as if they were upon shipboard. I know you will think this smells like a lie, but yet you shall have it. The islands were of a good length indeed, but not very high, containing about an hundred furlongs in compass; every one of these carried of those kind of men eight-and-twenty, of which some sat on either side of the island and rowed in their course with great cypress trees, branches, leaves and all, instead of oars. On the stern or hinder part, as I take it, stood the governor, upon a high hill, with a brazen rudder of a furlong in length in his hand: on the fore-part stood forty such fellows as those, armed for the fight, resembling men in all points but in their hair, which was all fire and burnt clearly, so that they needed no helmets. Instead of sails the wood growing in the island did serve their turns, for the wind blowing against it drave forward the island like a ship, and carried it which way the governor would have it, for they had pilots to direct them, and were as nimble to be stirred with oars as any long-boat. At the first we had the sight but of two or three of them: afterwards appeared no less than six hundred, which, dividing themselves in two parts, prepared for encounter, in which many of them by meeting with their barks together were broken in pieces, many were turned over and drowned: they that closed, fought lustily and would not easily be parted, for the soldiers in the front showed a great deal of valour, entering one upon another, and killed all they could, for none were taken prisoners. Instead of iron grapples they had mighty great polypodes fast tied, which they cast at the other, and if they once laid hold on the wood they made the isle sure enough for stirring. They darted and wounded one another with oysters that would fill a wain, and sponges as big as an acre. The leader on the one side was Æolocentaurus, and of the other Thalassopotes. The quarrel, as it seems, grew about taking a booty: for they said that Thalassopotes drave away many flocks of dolphins that belonged to Æolocentaurus, as we heard by their clamours one to another, and calling upon the names of their kings: but Æolocentaurus had the better of the day and sunk one hundred and fifty of the enemy's islands, and three they took with the men and all. The rest withdrew themselves and fled, whom the other pursued, but not far, because it grew towards evening, but returned to those that were wrecked and broken, which they also recovered for the most part, and took their own away with them: for on their part there were no less than fourscore islands drowned. Then they erected a trophy for a monument of this island fight, and fastened one of the enemy's islands with a stake upon the head of the whale. That night they lodged close by the beast, casting their cables about him, and anchored near unto him: their anchors are huge and great, made of glass, but of a wonderful strength. The morrow after, when they had sacrificed upon the top of the whale, and there buried their dead, they sailed away, with great triumph and songs of victory. And this was the manner of the islands' fight.

THE SECOND BOOK

Upon this we began to be weary of our abode in the whale, and our tarriance there did much trouble us. We therefore set all our wits a-work to find out some means or other to clear us from our captivity. First, we thought it would do well to dig a hole through his right side and make our escape that way forth, which we began to labour at lustily; but after we had pierced him five furlongs deep and found it was to no purpose, we gave it over. Then we devised to set the wood on fire, for that would certainly kill him without all question, and being once dead, our issue would be easy enough. This we also put in practice, and began our project at the tail end, which burnt seven days and as many nights before he had any feeling of our fireworks: upon the eighth and ninth days we perceived he began to grow sickly: for he gaped more dully than he was wont to do, and sooner closed his mouth again: the tenth and eleventh he was thoroughly mortified and began to stink: upon the twelfth day we bethought ourselves, though almost too late, that unless we underpropped his chops when he gaped next to keep them from closing, we should be in danger of perpetual imprisonment within his dead carcase and there miserably perish.

We therefore pitched long beams of timber upright within his mouth to keep it from shutting, and then made our ship in a readiness, and provided ourselves with store of fresh water, and all other things necessary for our use, Scintharus taking upon him to be our pilot, and the next morrow the whale died. Then we hauled our ship through the void passages, and fastening cables about his teeth, by little and little settled it into the sea, and mounting the back of the whale, sacrificed to Neptune, and for three days together took up our lodging hard by the trophy, for we were becalmed. The fourth day we put to sea, and met with many dead corpses that perished in the late sea-fight, which our ship hit against, whose bodies we took measure of with great admiration, and sailed for a few days in very temperate weather. But after that the north wind blew so bitterly that a great frost ensued, wherewith the whole sea was all frozen up, not only superficially upon the upper part, but in depth also the depth of four hundred fathoms, so that we were fain to forsake our ship and run upon the ice. The wind sitting long in this corner, and we not able to endure it, put this device in practice, which was the invention of Scintharus: — with mattocks and other instruments we made a mighty cave in the water, wherein we sheltered ourselves forty days together: in it we kindled fire, and fed upon fish, of which we found great plenty in our digging. At the last, our provision falling short, we returned to our frozen ship, which we set upright, and spreading her sails, went forward as well as if we had been upon water, leisurely and gently sliding upon the ice; but on the fifth day the weather grew warm, and the frost brake, and all was turned to water again. We had not sailed three hundred furlongs forwards but we came to a little island that was desert, where we only took in fresh water (which now began to fail us), and with our shot killed two wild bulls, and so departed. These bulls have their horns growing not upon their heads but under their eyes, as Momus thought it better. Then we entered into a sea, not of water but of milk, in which appeared a white island full of vines. This island was only a great cheese well pressed (as we afterwards found when we fed upon it), about some five-and-twenty furlongs in bigness: the vines were full of clusters of grapes, out of which we could crush no wine, but only milk: in the midst of the island there was a temple built dedicated to Galatea, one of the daughters of Nereus, as by the inscription appeared. As long as we remained there the soil yielded us food and victuals, and our drink was the milk that came out of the grapes: in these, as they said, reigneth Tyro, the daughter of Salmoneus, who, after her departure, received this guerdon at the hands of Neptune.

In this island we rested ourselves five days, and on the sixth put to sea again, a gentle gale attending us, and the seas all still and quiet. The eighth day, as we sailed onward, not in milk any longer, but in salt and azure water, we saw many men running upon the sea, like unto us every way forth, both in shape and stature, but only for their feet, which were of cork, whereupon, I suppose, they had the name of Phellopodes.

We marvelled much when we saw they did not sink, but keep above water, and travel upon it so boldly. These came unto us, and saluted us in the Grecian language, and said they were bound towards Phello, their own country, and for a while ran along by us, but at last turned their own way and left us, wishing us a happy and prosperous voyage. Within a while after many islands appeared, and near unto them, upon our left hand, stood Phello, the place whereunto they were travelling, which was a city seated upon a mighty great and round cork. Further off, and more towards the right hand, we saw five other islands, large and mountainous, in which much fire was burning; but directly before us was a spacious flat island, distant from us not above five hundred furlongs: and approaching somewhat near unto it, a wonderful fragrant air breathed upon us, of a most sweet and delicate smell, such as Herodotus, the story-writer, saith ariseth out of Arabia the happy, consisting of a mixture of roses, daffodils, gillyflowers, lilies, violets, myrtles, bays, and blossoms of vines: such a dainty odoriferous savour was conveyed unto us.

Being delighted with this smell, and hoping for better fortunes after our long labours, we got within a little of the isle, in which we found many havens on every side, not subject to overflowing, and yet of great capacity, and rivers of clear water emptying themselves easily into the sea, with meadows and herbs and musical birds, some singing upon the shore, and many upon the branches of trees, a still and gentle air compassing the whole country. When pleasant blasts gently stirred the woods the motion of the branches made a continual delightsome melody, like the sound of wind instruments in a solitary place: a kind of clamour also was heard mixed with it, yet not tumultuous nor offensive, but like the noise of a banquet, when some do play on wind instruments, some commend the music, and some with their hands applaud the pipe, or the harp. All which yielded us so great content that we boldly entered the haven, made fast our ship and landed, leaving in her only Scintharus and two more of our companions behind us. Passing along through a sweet meadow we met with the guards that used to sail about the island, who took us and bound us with garlands of roses (which are the strictest bands they have), to be carried to their governor: from them we heard, as we were upon the way, that it was the island of those that are called blessed, and that Rhadamanthus was governor there, to whom we were brought and placed the fourth in order of them that were to be judged.

The first trial was about Ajax, the son of Telamon, whether he were a meet man to be admitted into the society of the Heroes or not: the objections against him were his madness and the killing of himself: and after long pleading to and fro, Rhadamanthus gave this sentence, that for the present he should be put to Hippocrates, the physician of Cos, to be purged with helleborus, and upon the recovery of his wits to have admittance.

The second was a controversy of love, Theseus and Menelaus contending which had the better right to Helen; but Rh ad am an thus gave judgment on Menelaus' side, in respect of the manifold labours and perils he had incurred for that marriage' sake, whereas Theseus had wives enough beside to live withal—as the Amazon, and the daughters of Minos. The third was a question of precedency between Alexander, the son of Philip, and Hannibal, the Carthaginian, in which Alexander was preferred, and his throne placed next to the elder Cyrus the Persian.

In the fourth place we appeared, and he demanded of us what reason we had, being living men, to take land in that sacred country, and we told him all our adventures in order as they befell us: then he commanded us to stand aside, and considering upon it a great while, in the end proposed it to the benchers, which were many, and among them Aristides the Athenian, surnamed the Just: and when he was provided what sentence to deliver, he said that for our busy curiosity and needless travels we should be accountable after our death; but for the present we should have a time limited for our abode, during which we should feast with the Heroes and then depart, prefixing us seven months' liberty to conclude our tarriance, and no more. Then our garlands fell off from us of themselves, and we were set loose and led into the city to feast with the blessed.

The city was all of gold, compassed with a wall made of the precious stone smaragdus, which had seven gates, every one cut out of a whole piece of timber of cinnamon-tree: the pavement of the city and all the ground within the walls was ivory: the temples of all the gods are built of beryl, with large altars made all of one whole amethyst, upon which they offer their sacrifices: about the city runneth a river of most excellent sweet ointment, in breadth an hundred cubits of the larger measure, and so deep that a man may swim in it with ease. For their baths they have great houses of glass, which they warm with cinnamon: and their bathing-tubs are filled with warm dew instead of water. Their only garments are cobwebs of purple colour; neither have they any bodies, but are intactile and without flesh, a mere shape and presentation only: and being thus bodiless, they yet stand, and are moved, are intelligent, and can speak: and their naked soul seemeth to wander up and down in a corporal likeness: for if a man touch them not he cannot say otherwise, but that they have bodies, altogether like shadows standing upright, and not, as they are, of a dark colour. No man waxeth any older there than he was before, but of what age he comes thither, so he continues. Neither is there any night with them, nor indeed clear day: but like the twilight towards morning before the sun be up, such a kind of light do they live in. They know but one season of the year which is the spring, and feel no other wind but Zephyrus. The region flourisheth with all sorts of flowers, and with all pleasing plants fit for shade: their vines bear fruit twelve times a year, every month once: their pomegranate-trees, their apple-trees, and their other fruit, they say, bear thirteen times in the year, for in the month called Minous they bear twice. Instead of wheat their ears bear them loaves of bread ready baked, like unto mushrooms. About the city are three hundred three-score and five wells of water, and as many of honey, and five hundred of sweet ointment, for they are less than the other. They have seven rivers of milk and eight of wine.

They keep their feast without the city in a field called Elysium, which is a most pleasant meadow, environed with woods of all sorts, so thick that they serve for a shade to all that are invited, who sit upon beds of flowers, and are waited upon, and have everything brought unto them by the winds, unless it be to have the wine filled: and that there is no need of: for about the banqueting place are mighty great trees growing of clear and pure glass, and the fruit of those trees are drinking-cups and other kind of vessels of what fashion or greatness you will: and every man that comes to the feast gathers one or two of those cups, and sets them before him, which will be full of wine presently, and then they drink. Instead of garlands the nightingales and other musical birds gather flowers with their beaks out of the meadows adjoining, and flying over their heads with chirping notes scatter them among them.

They are anointed with sweet ointment in this manner: sundry clouds draw that unguent out of the fountains and the rivers, which settling over the heads of them that are at the banquet, the least blast of wind makes a small rain fall upon them like unto a dew. After supper they spend the time in music and singing: their ditties that are in most request they take out of Homer's verses, who is there present himself and feasteth among them, sitting next above Ulysses: their choirs consist of boys and virgins, which were directed and assisted by Eunomus the Locrian, and Arion the Lesbian, and Anacreon, and Stesichorus, who hath had a place there ever since his reconcilement with Helena. As soon as these have done there enter a second choir of swans, swallows, and nightingales; and when they have ended, the whole woods ring like wind-instruments by the stirring of the air.

But that which maketh most for their mirth are two wells adjoining to the banqueting place, the one of laughter, the other of pleasure: of these every man drinks to begin the feast withal, which makes them spend the whole time in mirth and laughter.

I will also relate unto you what famous men I saw in that association. There were all the demigods, and all that fought against Troy, excepting Ajax the Locrian: he only, they told me, was tormented in the region of the unrighteous. Of barbarians there was the elder and the younger Cyrus, and Anacharsis the Scythian, Zamolxis the Thracian, and Numa the Italian. There was also Lycurgus the

Lacedæmonian, and Phocion and Tellus the Athenians, and all the Wise Men, unless it were Periander.

I also saw Socrates, the son of Sophroniscus, prattling with Nestor and Palamedes, and close by him stood Hyacinthus the Lacedæmonian, and the gallant Narcissus and Hylas, and other beautiful and lovely youths, and for aught I could gather by him he was far in love with Hyacinthus, for he discoursed with him more than all the rest: for which cause, they said, Rhadamanthus was offended at him, and often threatened to thrust him out of the island if he continued to play the fool in that fashion, and not give over his idle manner of jesting, when he was at their banquet. Only Plato was not present, for they said he dwelled in a city framed by himself, observing the same rule of government and laws as he had prescribed for them to live under.

Aristippus and Epicurus are prime men amongst them, because they are the most jovial good fellows and the best companions. Diogenes the Sinopean was so far altered from the man he was before that he married with Lais the harlot, and was many times so drunk that he would rise and dance about the room as a man out of his senses. Æsop the Phrygian served them for a jester. There was not one Stoic in company but were still busied in ascending the height of virtue's hill: and of Chrysippus we heard that it was not lawful for him by any means to touch upon the island until he have the fourth time purged himself with helleborus. The Academics, they say, were willing enough to come, but that they yet are doubtful and in suspense, and cannot comprehend how there should be any such island; but indeed, I think, they were fearful to come to be judged by Rhadamanthus, because themselves have abolished all kind of judgment: yet many of them, they say, had a desire, and would follow after those that were coming hither, but were so slothful as to give it over because they were not comprehensive, and therefore turned back in the midst of their way.

These were all the men of note that I saw there; and amongst them all Achilles was held to be the best man, and next to him Theseus. For their manner of venery and copulation thus it is: they couple openly in the eyes of all men, both with females and male kind, and no man holds it for any dishonesty. Only Socrates would swear deeply that he accompanied young men in a cleanly fashion, and therefore every man condemned him for a perjured fellow: and Hyacinthus and Narcissus both confessed otherwise for all his denial.

The women there are all in common, and no man takes exception at it, in which respect they are absolutely the best Platonists in the world: and so do the boys yield themselves to any man's pleasure without contradiction.

After I had spent two or three days in this manner, I went to talk with Homer the poet, our leisure serving us both well, and to know of him what countryman he was, a question with us hard to be resolved, and he said he could not certainly tell himself, because some said he was of Chios, some of Smyrna, and many to be of Colophon; but he said indeed he was a Babylonian, and among his own countrymen not called Homer but Tigranes, and afterwards living as an hostage among the Grecians, he had therefore that name put upon him. Then I questioned him about those verses in his books that are disallowed as not of his making, whether they were written by him or not, and he told me they were all his own, much condemning Zenodotus and Aristarchus, the grammarians, for their weakness in judgment.

When he had satisfied me in this, I asked him again why he began the first verse of his poem with anger: and he told me it fell out so by chance, not upon any premeditation. I also desired to know of him whether he wrote his Odysseys before his Iliads, as many men do hold: but he said it was not so. As for his blindness which is charged upon him, I soon found it was far otherwise, and perceived it so plainly that I needed not to question him about it.

Thus was I used to do many days when I found him idle, and would go to him and ask him many questions, which he would give me answer to very freely: especially when we talked of a trial he had in the court of justice, wherein he got the better: for Thersites had preferred a bill of complaint against him for abusing him and scoffing at him in his Poem, in which action Homer was acquitted, having Ulysses for his advocate.

About the same time came to us Pythagoras the Samian, who had changed his shape now seven times, and lived in as many lives, and accomplished the periods of his soul. The right half of his body was wholly of gold; and they all agreed that he should have place amongst them, but were doubtful what to call him, Pythagoras or Euphorbus. Empedocles also came to the place, scorched quite over, as if his body had been broiled upon the embers; but could not be admitted for all his great entreaty.

The time passing thus along, the day of prizes for masteries of activity now approached, which they call Thanatusia. The setters of them forth were Achilles the fifth time, and Theseus the seventh time. To relate the whole circumstance would require a long discourse, but the principal points I will deliver. At wrestling Carus, one of the lineage of Hercules, had the best, and wan the garland from Ulysses. The fight with fists was equal between Arius the Ægyptian, who was buried at Corinth, and Epius, that combated for it. There was no prize appointed for the Pancratian fight: neither do I remember who got the best in running: but for poetry, though Homer without question were too good for them all, yet the best was given to Hesiodus. The prizes were all alike, garlands plotted of peacocks' feathers.

As soon as the games were ended, news came to us that the damned crew in the habitation of the wicked had broken their bounds, escaped the gaolers, and were coming to assail the island, led by Phalaris the Agrigentine, Busyris the Ægyptian, Diomedes the Thracian, Sciron, Pituocamptes, and others: which Rhadamanthus hearing, he ranged the Heroes in battle array upon the sea-shore, under the leading of Theseus and Achilles and Ajax Telamonius, who had now recovered his senses, where they joined fight; but the Heroes had the day, Achilles carrying himself very nobly. Socrates also, who was placed in the right wing, was noted for a brave soldier, much better than he was in his lifetime, in the battle at Delium: for when the enemy charged him, he neither fled nor changed countenance: wherefore afterwards, in reward of his valour, he had a prize set out for him on purpose, which was a beautiful and spacious garden, planted in the suburbs of the city, whereunto he invited many, and disputed with them there, giving it the name of Necracademia.

Then we took the vanquished prisoners, and bound them, and sent them back to be punished with greater torments.

This fight was also penned by Homer, who, at my departure, gave me the book to show my friends, which I afterwards lost and many things else beside: but the first verse of the poem I remember was this: "Tell me now, Muse, how the dead Heroes fought."

When they overcome in fight, they have a custom to make a feast with sodden beans, wherewith they banquet together for joy of their victory: only Pythagoras had no part with them, but sat aloof off, and lost his dinner because he could not away with beans.

Six months were now passed over, and the seventh halfway onwards, when a new business was begot amongst us. For Cinyras the son of Scintharus, a proper tall young man, had long been in love with Helena, and it might plainly be perceived that she as fondly doted upon him, for they would still be winking and drinking one to another whilst they were a-feasting, and rise alone together, and wander up and down in the wood. This humour increasing, and knowing not what course to take, Cinyras' device was to steal away Helena, whom he found as pliable to run away with him, to some of the islands adjoining, either to Phello, or Tyroessa, having before combined with three of the boldest fellows in my company to join with them in their conspiracy; but never acquainted his father with it, knowing that he would surely punish him for it.

Being resolved upon this, they watched their time to put it in practice: for when night was come, and I absent (for I was fallen asleep at the feast), they gave a slip to all the rest, and went away with Helena to shipboard as fast as they could. Menelaus waking about midnight, and finding his bed empty, and his wife gone, made an outcry, and calling up his brother, went to the court of Rhadamanthus.

As soon as the day appeared, the scouts told them they had descried a ship, which by that time was got far off into the sea. Then Rhadamanthus set out a vessel made of one whole piece of timber of asphodelus wood, manned with fifty of the Heroes to pursue after them, which were so willing on their way, that by noon they had overtaken them newly entered into the milky ocean, not far from Tyroessa, so near were they got to make an escape. Then took we their ship and hauled it after us with a chain of roses and brought it back again.

Rhadamanthus first examined Cinyras and his companions whether they had any other partners in this plot, and they confessing none, were adjudged to be tied fast by the privy members and sent into the place of the wicked, there to be tormented, after they had been scourged with rods made of mallows. Helena, all blubbered with tears, was so ashamed of herself that she would not show her face. They also decreed to send us packing out of the country, our prefixed time being come, and that we should stay there no longer than the next morrow: wherewith I was much aggrieved and wept bitterly to leave so good a place and turn wanderer again I knew not whither: but they comforted me much in telling me that before many years were past I should be with them again, and showed me a chair and a bed prepared for me against the time to come near unto persons of the best quality.

Then went I to Rhadamanthus, humbly beseeching him to tell me my future fortunes, and to direct me in my course; and he told me that after many travels and dangers, I should at last recover my country, but would not tell me the certain time of my return: and showing me the islands adjoining, which were five in number, and a sixth a little further off, he said, Those nearest are the islands of the ungodly, which you see burning all in a light fire, but the other sixth is the island of dreams, and beyond that is the island of Calypso, which you cannot see from hence. When you are past these, you shall come into the great continent, over against your own country, where you shall suffer many afflictions, and pass through many nations, and meet with men of inhuman conditions, and at length attain to the other continent.

When he had told me this, he plucked a root of mallows out of the ground, and reached it to me, commanding me in my greatest perils to make my prayers to that: advising me further neither to rake in the fire with my knife, nor to feed upon lupins, nor to come near a boy when he is past eighteen years of age: if I were mindful of this, the hopes would be great that I should come to the island again.

Then we prepared for our passage, and feasted with them at the usual hour, and next morrow I went to Homer, entreating him to do so much as make an epigram of two verses for me, which he did: and I erected a pillar of berylstone near unto the haven, and engraved them upon it. The epigram was this:

Lucian, the gods' belov'd, did once attain
To see all this, and then go home again.

After that day's tarrying, we put to sea, brought onward on our way by the Heroes, where Ulysses closely coming to me that Penelope might not see him, conveyed a letter into my hand to deliver to Calypso in the isle of Ogygia. Rhadamanthus also sent Nauplius, the ferryman, along with us, that if it were our fortune to put into those islands, no man should lay hands upon us, because we were bent upon other employments.

No sooner had we passed beyond the smell of that sweet odour but we felt a horrible filthy stink, like pitch and brimstone burning, carrying an intolerable scent with it as if men were broiling upon burning coals: the air was dark and muddy, from which distilled a pitchy kind of dew. We heard also the lash of the whips, and the roarings of the tormented: yet went we not to visit all the islands, but that wherein we landed was of this form: it was wholly compassed about with steep, sharp, and craggy rocks, without either wood or water: yet we made a shift to scramble up among the cliffs, and so went forwards in a way quite overgrown with briars and thorns through a most villainous ghastly country, and coming at last to the prison and place of torment we wondered to see the nature and quality of the soil, which brought forth no other flowers but swords and daggers, and round about it ran certain rivers, the first of dirt, the second of blood, and the innermost of burning fire, which was very broad and unpassable, floating like water, and working like the waves of the sea, full of sundry fishes, some as big as firebrands, others of a less size like coals of fire, and these they call Lychniscies.

There was but one narrow entrance into it, and Timon of Athens appointed to keep the door, yet we got in by the help of Nauplius, and saw them that were tormented, both kings and private persons very many, of which there were some that I knew, for there I saw Cinyras tied by private members, and hanging up in the smoke. But the greatest torments of all are inflicted upon them that told any lies in their lifetime, and wrote untruly, as Ctesias the Cnidian, Herodotus, and many other, which I beholding, was put in great hopes that I should never have anything to do there, for I do not know that ever I spake any untruth in my life. We therefore returned speedily to our ship (for we could endure the sight no longer), and taking our leaves of Nauplius, sent him back again.

A little after appeared the Isle of Dreams near unto us, an obscure country and unperspicuous to the eye, endued with the same quality as dreams themselves are: for as we drew, it still gave back and fled from us, that it seemed to be farther off than at the first, but in the end we attained it and entered the haven called Hypnus, and adjoined to the gate of ivory, where the temple of Alectryon stands, and took land somewhat late in the evening.

Entering the gate we saw many dreams of sundry fashions; but I will first tell you somewhat of the city, because no man else hath written any description of it: only Homer hath touched it a little, but to small purpose.

It is round about environed with a wood, the trees whereof are exceeding high poppies and mandragoras, in which an infinite number of owls do nestle, and no other birds to be seen in the island: near unto it is a river running, called by them Nyctiporus, and at the gates are two wells, the one named Negretus, the other Pannychia. The wall of the city is high and of a changeable colour, like unto the rainbow, in which are four gates, though Homer speak but of two: for there are two which look toward the fields of sloth, the one made of iron, the other of potter's clay, through which those dreams have passage that represent fearful, bloody, and cruel matters: the other two behold the haven and the sea, of which the one is made of horn, the other of ivory, which we went in at.

As we entered the city, on the right hand stands the temple of the Night, whom, with Alectryon, they reverence above all the gods: for he hath also a temple built for him near unto the haven. On the left hand stands the palace of sleep, for he is the sovereign king over them all, and hath deputed two great princes to govern under him, namely, Taraxion, the son of Matogenes, and Plutocles, the son of Phantasion.

In the middest of the market-place is a well, by them called Careotis, and two temples adjoining, the one of falsehood, the other of truth, which have either of them a private cell peculiar to the priests, and an oracle, in which the chief prophet is Antiphon, the interpreter of dreams, who was preferred by Sleep to that place of dignity.

These dreams are not all alike either in nature or shape, for some of them are long, beautiful, and pleasing: others again are as short and deformed. Some make show to be of gold, and others to be as base and beggarly. Some of them had wings, and were of monstrous forms: others set out in pomp, as it were in a triumph, representing the appearances of kings, gods, and other persons.

Many of them were of our acquaintance, for they had been seen of us before, which came unto us and saluted us as their old friends, and took us and lulled us asleep, and feasted us nobly and courteously, promising beside all other entertainment which was sumptuous and costly, to make us kings and princes. Some of them brought us home to our own country to show us our friends there, and come back with us the next morrow.

Thus we spent thirty days and as many nights among them, sleeping and feasting all the while, until a sudden clap of thunder awakened us all, and we starting up, provided ourselves of victuals, and took sea again, and on the third day landed in Ogygia. But upon the way I opened the letter I was to deliver, and read the contents, which were these:

"Ulysses to Calypso sendeth greeting. This is to give you to understand that after my departure from you in the vessel I made in haste for myself, I suffered shipwreck, and hardly escaped by the help of Leucothea into the country of the Phæacks, who sent me to mine own home, where I found many that were wooers to my wife, and riotously consumed my means; but I slew them all, and was afterwards killed myself by my son Telegonus, whom I begat of Circe, and am now in the island of the blessed, where I daily repent myself for refusing to live with you, and forsaking the immortality proffered me by you; but if I can spy a convenient time, I will give them all the slip and come to you."

This was the effect of the letter, with some addition concerning us, that we should have entertainment: and far had I not gone from the sea but I found such a cave as Homer speaks of, and she herself working busily at her wool. When she had received the letter, and brought us in, she began to weep and take on grievously, but afterwards she called us to meat, and made us very good cheer, asking us many questions concerning Ulysses and Penelope, whether she was so beautiful and modest as Ulysses had often before bragged of her.

And we made her such answer as we thought would give her best content: and departing to our ship, reposed ourselves near unto the shore, and in the morning put to sea, where we were taken with a violent storm, which tossed us two days together, and on the third we fell among the Colocynthopiratans. These are a wild kind of men, that issue out of the islands adjoining, and prey upon passengers, and for their shipping have mighty great gourds six cubits in length, which they make hollow when they are ripe, and cleanse out all that is within them, and use the rinds for ships, making their masts of reeds, and their sails of the gourd leaves.

These set upon us with two ships furnished and fought with us, and wounded many, casting at us instead of stones the seeds of those gourds. The fight was continued with equal fortune until about noon, at which time, behind the Colocynthopiratans, we espied the Caryonautans coming on, who, as it appeared, were enemies to the other, for when they saw them approach, they forsook us and turned about to fight with them; and in the mean space we hoist sail and away, leaving them together by the ears, and no doubt but the Caryonautans had the better of the day, for they exceeded in number, having five ships well furnished, and their vessels of greater strength, for they are made of nutshells cloven in the midst and cleansed, of which every half is fifteen fathom in length.

When we were got out of sight we were careful for the curing of our hurt men, and from that time forwards went no more unarmed, fearing continually to be assaulted on the sudden: and good cause we had: for before sun-setting some twenty men or thereabouts, which also were pirates, made towards us, riding upon monstrous great dolphins, which carried them surely: and when their riders gat upon their backs, would neigh like horses. When they were come near us, they divided themselves, some on the one side, and some on the other, and flung at us with dried cuttle-fishes and the eyes of sea-crabs: but when we shot at them again and hurt them, they would not abide it, but fled to the island, the most of them wounded.

About midnight, the sea being calm, we fell before we were aware upon a mighty great halcyon's nest, in compass no less than threescore furlongs, in which the halcyon herself sailed, as she was hatching her eggs, in quantity almost equalling the nest, for when she took her wings, the blast of her feathers had like to have overturned our ship, making a lamentable noise as she flew along.

As soon as it was day, we got upon it, and found it to be a nest, fashioned like a great lighter, with trees plaited and wound one within another, in which were five hundred eggs, every one bigger than a tun of Chios measure, and so near their time of hatching that the young chickens might be seen and began to cry. Then with an axe we hewed one of the eggs in pieces, and cut out a young one that had no feathers, which yet was bigger than twenty of our vultures.

When we had gone some two hundred furlongs from this nest, fearful prodigies and strange tokens appeared unto us, for the carved goose, that stood for an ornament on the stern of our ship, suddenly flushed out with feathers and began to cry. Scintharus, our pilot, that was a bald man, in an instant was covered with hair: and which was more strange than all the rest, the mast of our ship began to bud out with branches and to bear fruit at the top, both of figs and great clusters of grapes, but not yet ripe. Upon the sight of this we had great cause to be troubled in mind, and therefore besought the gods to avert from us the evil that by these tokens was portended.

And we had not passed full out five hundred furlongs, but we came in view of a mighty wood of pine-trees and cypress, which made us think it had been land, when it was indeed a sea of infinite depth, planted with trees that had no roots, but floated firm and upright, standing upon the water. When we came to it and found how the case stood with us, we knew not what to do with ourselves. To go forwards through the trees was altogether impossible: they were so thick and grew so close together: and to turn again with safety was as much unlikely.

I therefore got me up to the top of the highest tree to discover, if I could, what was beyond; and I found the breadth of the wood to be fifty furlongs or thereabout, and then appeared another ocean to receive us. Wherefore we thought it best to assay to lift up our ship upon the leaves of the trees which were thick grown, and by that means pass over, if it were possible, to the other ocean: and so we did: for fastening a strong cable to our ship, we wound it about the tops of the trees, and with much ado poised it up to the height, and placing it upon the branches, spread our sails, and were carried as it were upon the sea, dragging our ship after us by the help of the wind which set it forwards. At which time a verse of the poet Antimachus came to my remembrance, wherein he speaks of sailing over tops of trees.

When we had passed over the wood, and were come to the sea again, we let down our ship in the same manner as we took it up. Then sailed we forwards in a pure and clear stream, until we came to an exceeding great gulf or trench in the sea, made by the division of the waters as many times is upon land, where we see great clefts made in the ground by earthquakes and other means. Whereupon we struck sail and our ship stayed upon a sudden when it was at the pit's brim ready to tumble in: and we stooping down to look into it, thought it could be no less than a thousand furlongs deep, most fearful and monstrous to behold, for the water stood as it were divided into two parts, but looking on our right hand afar off, we perceived a bridge of water, which to our seeming, did join the two seas together and crossed over from the one to the other. Wherefore we laboured with oars to get unto it, and over it we went and with much ado got to the further side beyond all our expectation.

Then a calm sea received us, and in it we found an island, not very great, but inhabited with unsociable people, for in it were dwelling wild men named Bucephalians, that had horns on their heads like the picture of Minotaurus, where we went ashore to look for fresh water and victuals, for ours was all spent: and there we found water enough, but nothing else appeared; only we heard a great bellowing and roaring a little way off, which we thought to have been some herd of cattle, and going forwards, fell upon those men, who espying us, chased us back again, and took three of our company: the rest fled towards the sea.

Then we all armed ourselves, not meaning to leave our friends unrevenged, and set upon the Bucephalians as they were dividing the flesh of them that were slain, and put them all to flight, and pursued after them, of whom we killed fifty, and two we took alive, and so returned with our prisoners; but food we could find none.

Then the company were all earnest with me to kill those whom we had taken; but I did not like so well of that, thinking it better to keep them in bonds until ambassadors should come from the Bucephalians to ransom them that were taken, and indeed they did: and I well understood by the nodding of their heads, and their lamentable lowing, like petitioners, what their business was.

So we agreed upon a ransom of sundry cheeses and dried fish and onions and four deer with three legs apiece, two behind and one before. Upon these conditions we delivered those whom we had taken, and tarrying there but one day, departed.

Then the fishes began to show themselves in the sea, and the birds flew over our heads, and all other tokens of our approach to land appeared unto us. Within a while after we saw men travelling the seas, and a new found manner of navigation, themselves supplying the office both for ship and sailor, and I will tell you how. As they lie upon their backs in the water and their privy members standing upright, which are of a large size and fit for such a purpose, they fasten thereto a sail, and holding their cords in their hands, when the wind hath taken it, are carried up and down as please themselves.

After these followed others riding upon cork, for they yoke two dolphins together, and drive them on (performing themselves the place of a coachman), which draw the cork along after them. These never offered us any violence, nor once shunned our sight; but passed along in our company without fear, in a peaceable manner, wondering at the greatness of our ship, and beholding it on every side.

At evening we arrived upon a small island, inhabited, as it seemed, only by women, which could speak the Greek language; for they came unto us, gave us their hands, and saluted us, all attired like wantons, beautiful and young, wearing long mantles down to the foot: the island was called Cabbalusa and the city Hydramardia. So the women received us, and every one of them took aside one of us for herself, and made him her guest. But I pausing a little upon it (for my heart misgave me), looked narrowly round about, and saw the bones of many men, and the skulls lying together in a corner; yet I thought not good to make any stir, or to call my company about me, or to put on arms; but taking the mallow into my hand, made my earnest prayers thereto that I might escape out of those present perils.

Within a while after, when the strange female came to wait upon me, I perceived she had not the legs of a woman, but the hoofs of an ass. Whereupon I drew my sword, and taking fast hold of her, bound her, and examined her upon the point: and she, though unwillingly, confessed that they were sea-women, called Onosceleans, and they fed upon strangers that travelled that way. For, said she, when we have made them drunk, we go to bed to them, and in their sleep, make a hand of them.

I hearing this, left her bound in the place where she was, and went up to the roof of the house, where I made an outcry, and called my company to me, and when they were come together, acquainted them with all that I had heard, and showed them the bones, and brought them into her that was bound, who suddenly was turned into water, and could not be seen. Notwithstanding, I thrust my sword into the water to see what would come of it, and it was changed into blood.

Then we made all the haste we could to our ship, and got us away, and as soon as it was clear day, we had sight of the mainland, which we judged to be the country opposite to our continent. Whereupon we worshipped, and made our prayers, and took council what was now to be done. Some thought it best only to go a-land and so return back again: others thought it better to leave our ship there and march into the mid-land to try what the inhabitants would do: but whilst we were upon this consultation a violent storm fell upon us, which drave our ship against the shore, and burst it all in pieces, and with much ado we all swam to land with our arms, every man catching what he could lay hands on.

These are all the occurrences I can acquaint you withal, till the time of our landing, both in the sea, and in our course to the islands, and in the air, and after that in the whale; and when we came out again what betid unto us among the Heroes and among the dreams, and lastly among the Bucephalians and the Onosceleans. What passed upon land the next books shall deliver.

www.ingramcontent.com/pod-product-compliance
Lightning Source LLC
LaVergne TN
LVHW090040080526
838202LV00046B/3897